S0-BUA-816

Pirate Fun

Welcome aboard the *Corsair!*

You are a member of a pirate crew led by the dastardly Mad Jack Blackheart. Can you outwit the cutthroat captain and guide the crew to the buried treasure?

If you feel ready, turn the page to begin your pirate adventure. In each chapter you will find a swashbuckling challenge to overcome before you can move on to the next stage of your voyage.

Good luck!

First edition for the United States and Canada published in 2007
by Barron's Educational Series, Inc.

© 2006 Andromeda Children's Books,
An imprint of Pinwheel Ltd
Created and produced by Andromeda Children's Books,
An imprint of Pinwheel Ltd,
Winchester House, 259–269 Old Marylebone Road,
London, NW1 5XJ, UK

Author: Dominic Guard
Illustrator: Colin Howard
Art Director: Miranda Kennedy
Design: Arvind Shah and Patricia Hopkins
Managing Editor: Isabel Thomas
Production Director: Clive Sparling

All rights reserved. All inquiries should be addressed to:
Barron's Educational Series, Inc.
250 Wireless Boulevard, Hauppauge, New York 11788
www.barronseduc.com

ISBN-13: 978-0-7641-9343-9
ISBN-10: 0-7641-9343-0
Library of Congress Control Number: 2006932205

Printed in China
9 8 7 6 5 4 3 2 1

Contents

All Aboard!

At the end of the summer you are standing in a little harbor. The sun shines brilliantly, and gulls glide over the bright blue ocean on a warm south wind.

Suddenly, the wind changes direction and blows hard from the North. A murky mist rolls in, and you can barely see the end of your nose. You feel something lurking behind you, and a voice bellows in your ear:

"The summer is over for you, young sprog! You're press-ganged!" And with that, two huge hands grab you and drag you toward the misty ocean!

"I'm the wrong person! You've got the wrong person!" you shout in terror.

The booming voice laughs back, "The wrong person, eh? Excellent! I likes wrong people— they make great pirates!"

You can't quite believe your eyes as the mist clears to reveal an enormous pirate ship.

Polly falls silent with fear as sneering pirates join you on the deck of the ship, running hither and thither as the captain barks out his orders.

"I hates land! I hates everything, I does! Now set the mainsail and let the wind take her!"

You find yourself sailing out to sea bound for who knows where. Although you are surrounded by a gang of pirates, you have never felt so alone. You are not at all sure if you like being just one more Jack! The pirates are eyeing you suspiciously—you don't fit in very well.

> Search your Pirate Pack for things to help you blend in. An eye patch, dagger, and parrot are perfect!

Mad Jack Blackheart

"Mad Jack Blackheart's me name and you, Jack, will be me cabin boy!" The parrot upon his shoulder puts its wings over its ears, so cruel and terrible is the pirate captain's voice. As you are bundled aboard the ship, you shout out once more, "You've got the wrong person! My name's not Jack!"

"He calls everyone Jack! He calls me Jack and my name's Polly!" squawks the parrot. "I hates birds, I do!" screams Mad Jack as he fires his pistols at passing gulls.

Pirate Speak

With your eye patch, dagger, and Polly the parrot on your shoulder, you feel more like part of the crew.

As you climb into your hammock you ask, "Polly, do you think I'm fitting in?" But Polly replies, "Best call me Jack. We're all Jacks here!"

"Why does he call everyone Jack?" you ask. "Well it's a long story," Polly replies, "but Mad Jack is really called Cuthbert. His terrible father, Madder Jack Blackheart, cared so little for his children that he couldn't be bothered to learn their names.

He called them all Jack. Now Mad Jack calls everyone Jack and doesn't care for anyone."

"And where are we going?" you ask.

"We're looking for the treasure that was burie long ago by Madder Jack—he hid it from Mad Jack," explains Polly. "Mad Jack's got a map, and all we know is that it's buried on an island in an archipelago."

"An arkie-pelly what?" you ask.

"It's a group of little islands" explains Polly. "As it's your first voyage, I'll get you a book to help you with pirate words. And be sure to wea your dagger at all times—never trust a pirate!" With that, Polly flies off and returns with a huge dusty book in his claws.

Shiver me timbers!

The dictionary Polly has given you is a great help. People have spent weeks on a pirate ship without understanding a word!

As you learn all the words, you notice that there aren't many kind ones. This could be a pretty horrible voyage! You are pleased to have a bucko like Polly on board.

Archipelago
Group of islands

Arrrgh!
Word put before anything to sound scary

Avast!
Stop!

Aye
Yes

Belay there!
Stop very quickly!

Bilge!
Disgusting water at the bottom of the ship; means rubbish

Blimey!
What a surprise!

Booty
Anything pirates like to steal

Briny
The ocean

Bucko
A friend (like Polly!)

Clap of thunder
A strong drink

Crow's nest
A very high lookout on a ship's mast

Deadlights
Eyes

Doubloons
Very precious gold coins that pirates count often

Gangway!
Get out of my way!

Jack
Everyone

Jolly Roger
The pirates' flag of a skull and crossbones

Hang the jib
Looking angrier than usual

Hearties
Friends

Hornswaggle
To cheat

Landlubber
Someone who doesn't like the sea

Me
My

Mess
A meal

Messdeck
A show-off, someone who has a meal

Mutineer
A sailor who has had enough of a Squiffy Captain

Oggin
The Sea

Press-ganged
To be stolen and taken to sea

Scallywag
A pretty bad pirate

Scurvy
Disgusting

Shanty
A song

Shiver me timbers!
What a big surprise!

Sink me!
An even bigger surprise!

Smartly
Quickly

Spiffing!
Excellent!

Sprogs
Children

Squiffy
A very, very bad pirate

Swab
A completely and utterly useless pirate

Walk the plank
To be made to walk off the ship into the sea

Ye
You

Yo-ho-ho!
I'm having a very good time!

Stargazing

One very dark night, a long time ago, Mad Jack was pacing the deck of the *Corsair*, trying to work out how his compass worked.

It once belonged to his father, Madder Jack Blackheart, who could not understand it either. On this particular night, when hopelessly lost, Mad Jack flew into a rage and threw the old compass into the sea, shouting: "Aaargh, me compass is hopeless!

Avast! I'll not even let it walk the plank—it's straight into the oggin for it!" He didn't regret losing his compass, because Blackhearts don't want help from anyone or anything. Now he tries to guide the *Corsair* by the sun, moon, and stars.

Navigating at night

Because Captain Blackheart is so hopeless at navigation, he gives the job to you. But you have never navigated before! The cruel captain couldn't care less and orders you to:

"Move smartly sprog and don't be a swab! Keeps the North Star on your right and we'll be right! Then we'll be going where we wants to! Otherwise I'll hang the jib and makes you walk the plank!"

But listen carefully. No star is really fixed in its position, because we live in a universe that is never still. Everything is moving in some direction or other, and many big groups of stars are rotating. You begin to spot shapes in the night sky. You recognize all the famous star constellations: The Great Bear, The Lion, the Twins… and then you spot a constellation you've never heard of! It seems to suggest that the treasure lies in that direction. You must be good at navigation after all!

Find a dark place and look carefully at the constellations. Can you spot the one that might lead to the treasure?

Quest for the Compass

You tell Mad Jack to head toward the treasure chest in the stars, but he ignores you. Polly says that Mad Jack prefers to be lost. Getting lost makes him angry, and the angrier he is, the more scared his crew is, so the better he feels!

The *Corsair* sails around and around in circles, making you and Polly as dizzy as sea dogs chasing their tails.

As the salty sea spray splatters your face, Polly sits upon your shoulder and comforts you with a tale about a mutineer who tried to shoot Mad Jack with a pistol.

Unfortunately, the mutineer, who didn't have very good eyesight, missed the captain and shot straight through one of the doubloons that he was counting at the time. The mutineer was forced to walk the plank, and the doubloon was made into an earring to remind the crew that it is very difficult to get rid of Mad Jack.

The missing compass

Polly knows where Mad Jack keeps the earring, so you set off down to the captain's cabin to see it. Inside a leaky wooden chest you find the earring and a pile of old compasses in different colors and sizes.

> Hold the earring in your pack over each compass. The one that fits exactly will help you find the treasure.

"Shiver me timbers!" Polly squawks, "It's Mad Jack's missing compass!"

"It wasn't lost after all!" you cry. You are delighted because you now own the most useful sailor's tool of all. Compasses always point to the North, so you will always know which way you are going. Perhaps now Mad Jack will listen to your directions.

You quickly slip the compass into your pocket and put the earring on. But as you are about to leave Mad Jack's cabin, you hear heavy footsteps outside the door.

"Sink me! It's Mad Jack!" you whisper, but Polly has hidden, leaving you to face him alone!

The Captain's Cabin

One of the most disgusting jobs aboard the *Corsair* is keeping Mad Jack clean. Although he looks like an adult, he can't look after himself at all. As he storms into his cabin, you have no choice but to say you are there on cleaning duty!

You must wash Mad Jack's fishy hands, brush his rotten teeth, scrub his sickening socks, and polish his boots with bilge water. The worst job of all is combing the maggots out of Mad Jack's beard.

As you set to work, you glance around the room and notice a picture of the captain as a young boy. You try hard not to snicker. Next to the picture, there is a strange inscription carved into the wooden wall. Bravely, you ask Mad Jack what the inscription means. But he doesn't like to be asked questions, and shouts at you:

Captain Morgan steered his crew
'cross the briny bright and blue.
All mean pirates
through and through
would follow their captain
hard and true.

But life at sea is oh so boring.
By mid morning
they were roaring.
So they took up their own
steering,
to try their hand at mutineering.

"Arrrgh! Why should I know what it means,
you little scallywag? I don't have no time for
no reading!" Then the cunning captain asks:
"I don't supposes ye can reads it, can ye?"

Mysterious words

You read the rhyme aloud, but you still don't
understand it. Mad Jack is disappointed, but
he seems pleased that you can't understand
the weaselly words either. Then, without
warning, the cruel captain dozes off.

When Mad Jack starts snoring, Polly appears
from his hiding place under the bed. He suggests
that you use the skull on the mantelpiece to help
you read the inscription properly.

"How will that help?" you ask. You are still
annoyed that Polly abandoned you. "Trust me,
me hearty!" replies Polly, "but be very careful
not to wake Mad Jack!"

Place the skull from your pack
over the shadow on the inscription to
read the clue.

Master the Map

Suddenly smelly old Mad Jack wakes with a start and shouts: "What's that I hear? Do I hear hornswaggling? I always fights hornswagglers! Don't lets anyone think I don't know what's going on!"

This is the first time you had considered that Blackheart might know what is going on! But you think it is best to say nothing to the captain about the hidden message.

"If you two won't argue with me, I'll go up on deck and argue with me crew," he roars. As Mad Jack climbs to the deck, you hear him calling out: "You can either fight me or walk the plank!" This sounds like a very difficult choice, and you are pleased you don't have to make it.

While Blackheart is bullying his crew, you seize the chance to look around the cabin again, and spot a map spread out on the captain's table.

A hidden clue

"Mad Jack's father drew that map," Polly explains. "It's Double X Archipelago, where the treasure is buried!" Polly tells you that Mad Jack can't understand the strange squiggles at the bottom of the map. You suddenly remember the inscription that told you to "Master the map with a mirror." You start to hunt around the cabin excitedly.

"What are you doing?" Polly squawks. "It's a clue!" you shout back. "Help me find a mirror!" It takes a long time because Mad Jack hates looking in mirrors.

The map is hidden in your Pirate Pack! Use a small mirror to decipher the writing, then follow instructions

"Be quick! He's coming!" shouts Polly. You look up to see Mad Jack glaring through his cabin window at you and yelling: "What's you doing you swabby sprog? No one messes with me map! I'm the captain and only I can touch it because only I understands it!"

15

Follow the Flags

There is so much mess in Mad Jack's cabin that you have the perfect excuse. "Aye-aye, Captain!" you reply. "I was only dusting it so that you would see it a bit better."

From now on, whenever the captain is bullying his crew on deck, you explore his cabin for clues. Since Mad Jack nearly caught you with the map, Polly always keeps a lookout to tell you when he might return.

One day, you find two very dusty books hidden under the captain's bed. One is titled SEMAPHORE and the other FLAG CODES. Surely Mad Jack doesn't use the books.

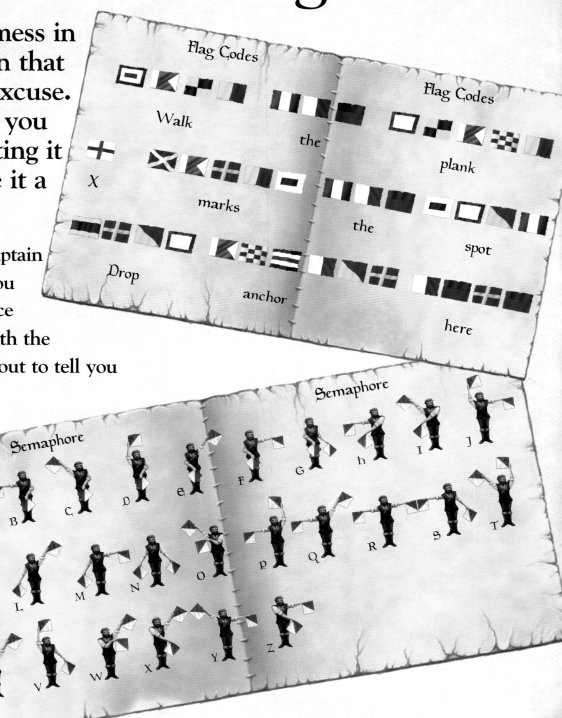

A sailor's code

Polly tells you that Blackheart stole the books from another ship long ago, but as they didn't contain any pictures of treasure maps, he lost interest in them. "What's semaphore anyway?" you ask Polly.

"I don't know what sema's for; I don't even know what sema *is*," the parrot replies.

As you flick through the books, you realize that they are both flag codes. "Semaphore is a way of sending messages with flags!" you shout. "Shhhh, Mad Jack'll hear you shouting, and he hates people stealing anything he has stolen," Polly whispers.

Bravely, you decide to smuggle the books out of the cabin and hide them under your hammock, hoping the captain won't notice anything is missing from his messy cabin.

It is very hard to sleep in a hammock. When the sea is rough, you fall out all the time. If you do manage to doze off, you are woken by the loud crashes of other pirates falling out of their hammocks! But that night, every time you fall out, you sneak a look at your hidden semaphore and flag books.

Study the open books carefully. Your decoding skills will come in handy on your quest!

17

X Marks the Spot

As you wake the next morning, you look out of your porthole and spot a dry desert island with nothing on it but four drooping palm trees.

You smile as you realize that the palm trees make the shape of two Xs. This must be the first island in the Double X Archipelago! The hidden writing on Mad Jack's map told you that the treasure lies to the east. Only you can tell the helmsman (the pirate who steers the ship) to head to the east, as you are the only person on board who can read a compass. You are worried that Blackheart will be angry if you talk to the helmsman—but if you find the treasure, maybe he will be happy enough to let you go home.

You ask Polly to distract Blackheart. While the parrot tells the captain how brave and brilliant he is, you quietly tell the helmsman to travel toward the east. He is so dizzy that he is happy to go in any direction as long as it's in a straight line.

A sinister shipwreck

As you leave the helmsman, you overhear him saying: "That young sprog with the compass knows what he is doing. I smells treasure!"
You wonder what treasure smells like and hope you do know what you are doing! Several sea miles later, you sail past a ship wrecked upon a rocky island. Could this be your next clue? Flags are fluttering from the ship's mast, and a ragged old man is jumping up and down waving more flags at you.

Use the semaphore alphabet and flag codes to decode the messages from the shipwrecked man.

Bird's-Eye View

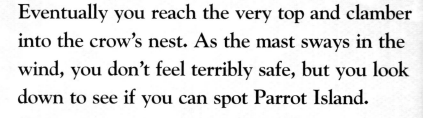

The crow's nest is at the top of the very high ship's mast. Just gazing up there makes you dizzy! Slowly and carefully you climb the ragged rope ladder, past gliding gulls and misty, wispy clouds.

Eventually you reach the very top and clamber into the crow's nest. As the mast sways in the wind, you don't feel terribly safe, but you look down to see if you can spot Parrot Island.

Polly flies up and joins you in the crow's nest, squawking: "Did you know that on the deck you see a horizon that is three miles away, but from the crow's nest, you can see for 12 miles?"

"But all I can see is lots of little islands—how am I supposed to know which one is Parrot Island?" you ask miserably.

Madder Jack's Map

Suddenly you remember Madder Jack Blackheart's treasure map—perhaps that has more clues! "Quick, Polly, get me the map!" you ask. Polly flies down to the captain's cabin, where Mad Jack is sleeping, and slowly pulls the treasure map from his heavy hands.

You start to compare the map to the archipelago in front of you. Using your compass, you look for Parrot Island to the east, but you can't see it anywhere.

Then Polly tells you that Madder Jack Blackheart always drew his mad maps upside down. You turn the map upside down. Sure enough, you spot a parrot-shaped island in the east!

Polly flies down to tell the helmsman which island to head for. As you study the upside-down map, you notice more of the strange writing. It must be another clue!

Use a mirror to read the writing in the sea chart below, and decode the message.

South, East, Southeast, North,
Northeast, Northwest, East, West ~ East, Southeast,
Northeast, South, Northeast ~ North, South ~ East, North,
South, Northeast ~ South, East, West, Southeast

Treasure Trove!

When you arrive at Parrot Island, Mad Jack is still dozing. The crew follows you ashore, their eyes glinting wickedly at the thought of the treasure.

But what do you do now? You can't see a rat anywhere. You sit down wearily on a rock that looks like a skull. The cruel crew gathers behind you and grumbles that you don't know what to do next.

Suddenly you spot some writing scratched into the skull-shaped rock:

4 steps north
7 steps east
4 steps south
3 steps west
8 steps north
3 steps east

On the trail

Starting from the rock, you follow the directions using your compass. The crew trails behind you, mumbling and moaning that you will never find anything. They have been disappointed so many times by Blackheart that they gave up hope of finding treasure long ago!

Line up North on the compass with north on the map. Each grid square equals one step. Follow the directions, then lift the flap to see if you are right!

Treasure hoard

You arrive at a tall, drooping palm tree. Revolting rats are crawling around underneath it. The whole crew starts digging into the sand—and guess what! They find bags stuffed with golden doubloons!

"Well done! Well done! Well done!" squawks Polly. The crew starts dancing a jig as they sing this pirate shanty:

We wish that we weren't all called Jack,
We wish we had our freedom back!
Blackheart's squiffy, he's a swab,
He's really hopeless at his job.
We dream of stealing all his treasure,
And his cutlass for good measure.
Make the cabin boy our captain,
Better things will surely happen!
The cabin boy is really clever,
We'll follow him through storms forever!

Suddenly you hear a booming voice and look up to see Mad Jack heading toward you, looking furious.

23

From Cabin Boy to Captain

Y ou expect the crew to hide, but instead they surround Mad Jack and tie him to a tree!

The crew gives you the captain's hat and you cry out: "Shiver me timbers! We've got the booty, me hearties! Set sail for home!"

Use the bag of doubloons in your Pirate Pack to learn Polly's tricks. After all, what's the point of being a pirate captain if you have to be completely good...

The crew heads back toward the *Corsair*. You feel bad for leaving Blackheart tied to the tree, so you smear the ropes with honey, hoping that the rats will chew through them after you have gone. As you head home with the treasure, Polly shows you some hornswaggling tricks that every pirate captain should know!

Honey